Peter
and the
Magic
Goose

and other magical stories

Compiled by Vic Parker

Miles Kelly

First published in 2012 by Miles Kelly Publishing Ltd
Harding's Barn, Bardfield End Green, Thaxted, Essex, CM6 3PX, UK

2 4 6 8 10 9 7 5 3 1

Publishing Director Belinda Gallagher
Creative Director Jo Cowan
Editorial Director Rosie McGuire
Editor Carly Blake
Senior Designer Joe Jones
Editorial Assistant Lauren White
Production Manager Elizabeth Collins
Reprographics Anthony Cambray, Stephan Davis, Jennifer Hunt

ISBN 978-1-84810-582-9

Printed in China

British Library Cataloguing-in-Publication Data
A catalogue record for this book is available from the British Library

ACKNOWLEDGEMENTS

The publishers would like to thank the following artists who have contributed to this book:
Cover: Lesley Danson at The Bright Agency
Advocate Art: Alida Massari
The Bright Agency: Marcin Piwowarski, Tom Sperling
Marsela Hajdinjak

All other artwork from the Miles Kelly Artwork Bank

The publishers would like to thank the following sources for the use of their photographs:
Shutterstock: (page decorations) Dragana Francuski Tolimir
Dreamstime: (frames) Gordan

Every effort has been made to acknowledge the source and copyright holder of each picture.
Miles Kelly Publishing apologises for any unintentional errors or omissions.

Made with paper from a sustainable forest

www.mileskelly.net   info@mileskelly.net

www.factsforprojects.com

Contents

The Hermit   4

The Elf and
the Housewife   15

The Paradise
of Children   18

Peter and the
Magic Goose   29

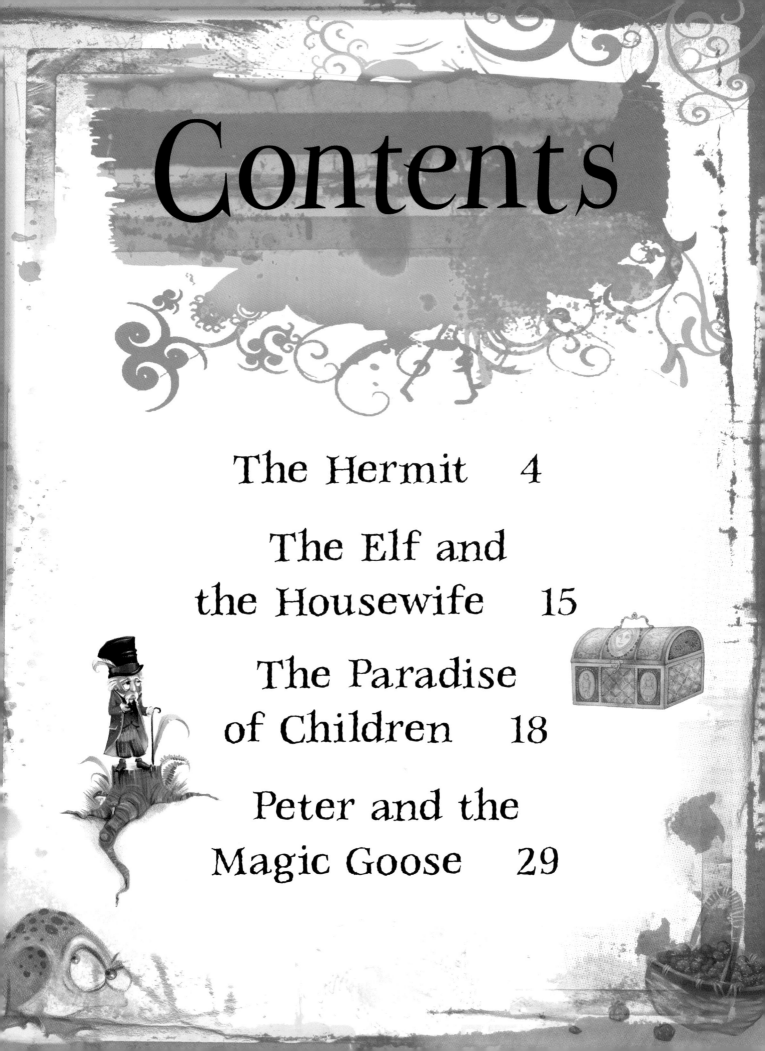

The Hermit

From *Tales of Wonder Every Child Should Know*
by Kate Douglas Wiggin and
Nora Archibald Smith

IN THE REIGN of King Moabdar there lived at Babylon a young man named Zadig. He was handsome, rich, and good-hearted. At the moment when this story opens, he was travelling to see the world and learn wisdom. However, he had seen so many terrible disasters and encountered so much misery among people that he had begun to think that the world was very unfair and to doubt that God existed. In this very unhappy state of mind he was walking on the banks of the River Euphrates, when he chanced to meet a holy hermit, whose snowy beard fell to his belt. He carried a scroll which he was reading very intently. Zadig stopped, bowed, and inquired what the scroll was.

"It is the Book of Destiny," replied the hermit. "Would you like to read it?"

He handed it to Zadig, but though Zadig knew a dozen languages, he could not understand a word of it. His curiosity increased.

"I can tell from your face that you are a troubled man," said the kindly hermit.

"Alas!" said Zadig. "I do feel very gloomy."

"Allow me to accompany you," said the hermit, "I may be useful to you. I am sometimes able to comfort the sorrowful."

Zadig was impressed by the holy appearance and the mysterious scroll of the old hermit, and thought that he must be very learned and wise. He was delighted that the old man wanted to accompany him. As they walked, the hermit spoke of fairness, of fate, of temptations and human weaknesses, and of all the goodness in life, with so much power that Zadig was quite captivated and wanted to listen to him for as long as possible. He begged the hermit not to leave him until they returned to Babylon.

"I ask you the same favour," said the hermit. "Promise me that, whatever I may do, you will keep me company for several days."

Zadig gave the promise, and they journeyed onwards together.

That night the travellers arrived at a grand mansion. The hermit begged for food and lodging

for himself and his companion. The porter, who was so richly dressed that he might have been mistaken for a prince, ushered them in with a very snooty air. The chief servant showed them the magnificent apartments where they were to spend the night, and they were then admitted to the great hall to dine at the long, long dinner table – albeit they were sat at the very bottom, where the master of the mansion did not even cast a glance at them. They were, however, served with all sorts of delicious morsels, and, after dinner, washed their hands in a golden

basin set with emeralds and rubies. After an extremely comfortable night's sleep, the next morning, before they left the castle, a servant brought them each a piece of gold.

"The master of the house," said Zadig, as they went their way, "appears to be a generous man, although he obviously thinks too highly of himself." As he spoke he noticed that a kind of large pouch that the hermit carried appeared much bigger than usual. He asked what was in it and the hermit explained that it was the golden basin, set with precious stones, which he had stolen! Zadig was highly astonished – but he didn't say anything.

At noon the hermit stopped before a little house, in which lived a man who was very wealthy but very mean. An old valet in a shabby coat received them very rudely, showed them into the stable, and set before them a few rotten olives, some mouldy bread, and beer which had turned sour. However, the hermit didn't seem upset at all. In fact, he ate and drank with as much content as he had shown the night before. Then, addressing the old valet, who had kept his eye upon them to make sure that they stole nothing, he gave him the two gold pieces which they had received that morning, and thanked him for his kind attention. "Be so good," he added, "as to let me see your master."

The astonished valet showed them in.

"Most mighty sir," said the hermit, "I can only give you my humble thanks for the noble manner in which you have received us. I beseech you to accept this golden basin as a token of my gratitude."

The mean man almost fell backwards with amazement. The hermit, without waiting for him to recover, set off with speed with his companion.

"What does all this mean?" asked Zadig. "You steal a golden basin set with jewels from a man who receives you generously, and you give it to a curmudgeon who treats you badly."

"My son," replied the hermit, "I can assure you

that from now on, the mighty lord who only welcomes travellers in order to display his riches, will grow wiser. However, the mean man will gradually be taught generosity. Be amazed at nothing, and follow me."

Zadig knew not whether he was dealing with the most foolish or the wisest of all men. But the hermit spoke with such faith that Zadig had no choice except to follow him.

That night they came to a simple, comfortable-looking house, with no signs of either showiness nor meanness. The owner was a wise man who had taken himself off to live by himself and study peacefully the rules of goodness and common sense, and who yet was happy and contented. He had built this calm house to suit himself, and he received the strangers in it with openness. He led them himself to a comfortable chamber, where he left the travellers to rest awhile. Then he returned to lead them to a dainty little supper. They held an interesting conversation, during which they all agreed that the wisest people are not always the ones in charge of the things that happen in the world. The hermit also made the point that the world is much bigger than we know and things often happen for reasons which we don't understand. Zadig wondered how a person who committed such mad acts could seem to talk so sensibly!

At length, the host led the two travellers to their apartment, and thanked heaven for sending him two visitors who were so wise and good. He offered them some money, but the old man declined with thanks and bade their host goodnight.

At break of day the hermit woke his comrade. "We must be going," he remarked. "But while everyone is still asleep, I wish to leave this worthy man a gift." With these words he took a torch and set the house on fire. Zadig burst forth into cries of horror, and would have stopped the frightful act, but the hermit was somehow stronger and pushed him away. Beaten back by both the old man and the heat, Zadig was forced to leave the house in a blaze and retreat to a safe distance. When the travellers were both a good way off, the hermit looked back calmly at the burning pile. "Heaven be praised!" he cried. "Our kind host's house is destroyed." At these words Zadig knew not whether he should burst out laughing, call the holy man an old rascal, knock him down, or run away. Still overwhelmed by the firm manner of the hermit, he followed him to their next lodging.

This was the dwelling of a charitable widow, who had a nephew of fourteen, her only hope and joy. She did her best to treat the travellers well, and next morning she bade her nephew guide them safely past a bridge, which had become dangerous to cross. The youth led the way. "Come," said the hermit, when they were half across the bridge,

"I must show my gratitude toward your aunt," and as he spoke he seized the young man and threw him into the river. The youth fell and was swallowed by the torrent.

"Oh, monster!" exclaimed Zadig.

"You promised me more patience," said the old man. "Listen! Beneath the ruins of that house which I set on fire, the owner will find treasure, while this young man, whose existence I cut short, would have turned to wickedness and killed his aunt within a year, and yourself in two."

"Who told you so?" cried Zadig. "Even if you read this in your Book of Destiny, who bestowed on you the power to drown a youth who never hurt you?"

Once he had spoken, he saw that the old man had a beard no longer, and that his face had become young. His hermit's frock had disappeared, and four white wings covered his back and shone with light.

"You are an angel of heaven!" cried Zadig.

"People," replied the angel Jezrael, for that's who he was "judge all things without true knowledge, and you, of all people, most deserved help to become wise. The world imagines that the youth who has just died fell by accident into the water, and that by similar accident the rich man's house was set on fire. But there is no such thing as chance — everything happens to test people or to punish people or because of things which must happen in the future."

As he spoke, the angel flew up to heaven, and Zadig fell upon his knees.

The Elf and the Housewife

Juliana Horatia Gatty Ewing

THERE ONCE LIVED a penny-pinching Housewife and one day an elf came knocking at her door.

"Can you lend us a saucepan?" said he. "There's a wedding in the hill, and all the pots are in use."

The Housewife went to get one, but she thought to herself: 'I'll give him the old one. It leaks, and the elves are such nimble workers, they are sure to mend it. So I'll help the elves and at the same time I'll save the sixpence that the tinker would have charged me to repair it.'

She gave the old saucepan to the dwarf, who thanked her, and went away.

In due time the saucepan was returned, and, as the Housewife had foreseen, it was neatly mended. At supper-time she filled the pan with milk, and set it on the fire to warm for the children's supper. But in only a few minutes the milk was so burned and smoked that no one could touch it.

"Oh how infuriating!" cried the Housewife, almost crying at the waste. "There's a whole quart of good milk wasted!"

"And that's sixpence," cried a voice from the chimney. "You didn't save the money after all!"

And with that the elf himself came tumbling down the chimney, and went off laughing through the door.

But from that day forwards, the saucepan was as good as any other.

The Paradise of Children

From *A Wonder-Book for Girls and Boys*
by Nathaniel Hawthorne

LONG, LONG AGO, there was a boy named Epimetheus who didn't have a best friend – until he met a girl called Pandora. The first time Pandora went to Epimetheus's house, she noticed a curious, great box. And almost the first question she put to him, after crossing the threshold, was: "Epimetheus, what have you in that box?"

"That is a secret," answered Epimetheus, "and you must not ask any questions about it. The box was left here to be kept safely, and I do not myself know what it contains."

"But who gave it to you?" asked Pandora. "And where did it come from?"

"That is a secret, too," replied Epimetheus.

"How vexing!" exclaimed Pandora, pouting.

"Oh, come, don't think of it any more," cried Epimetheus. "Let's go and play with the other children."

It is thousands of years since Epimetheus and Pandora were alive, and the world, nowadays, is very different from in their time. Then, everybody was a child. They needed no fathers and mothers because there was no danger, nor trouble of any kind, and no clothes to be mended, and there was always plenty to eat and drink. It was a very pleasant life indeed. No jobs to be done, no schoolwork to be studied – there was nothing but games and dancing and singing and laughter. For what was most wonderful of all, the children never quarrelled or cried or sulked. The truth is, those ugly little winged monsters, called Troubles, which are now almost as numerous as mosquitoes, had never yet been seen on the earth. It is probable that the very greatest annoyance which a child had ever experienced was Pandora's vexation at not being able to discover the secret of the mysterious box. This was at first only the faint shadow of a Trouble, but every day it grew more and more.

"Where can the box have come from?" Pandora continually kept saying to herself. "And what in the world can be inside it?" One day she begged Epimetheus to tell her more about how the box came to be in his house.

"It was just left at the door," replied Epimetheus, "by a person dressed in an odd kind of a cloak, and a cap that seemed to be made partly of feathers, so that it looked almost as if it had wings. He had a curious walking staff – it was like two serpents twisting around a stick, and was carved so naturally that I, at first, thought the serpents were alive. He told me very sternly that until he comes back and gives permission, no one has any right to lift the lid of the box."

Then, quite fed up of thinking about the box, Epimetheus went out to play.

Pandora, who had refused to go with him, was left gazing at the box. It was made of a beautiful kind of wood, so highly polished that she could see her face in it. The edges and corners were carved with most wonderful skill. There were figures of graceful men and women, and the prettiest children ever seen, surrounded by a tangle of flowers and leaves. Once or twice as Pandora examined it, she fancied that she saw a face not so lovely, or something or other that was disagreeable. Nevertheless, on looking more closely, and touching the spot with her finger, she could discover nothing of the kind.

The most beautiful face of all was in the centre of the lid. Pandora thought that, had it been able to speak, it looked just as if it would have said: "Do not be afraid, Pandora! What harm can there be in opening the box? Never mind that poor, simple Epimetheus! You are wiser than he, and have ten times as much spirit. Open the box, and see if you do not find something very pretty!"

The box was fastened by a very intricate knot of gold cord. There appeared to be no end to this knot, and no beginning. But Pandora was not one to give up easily. She stood for a while, turning it this way and that, and then murmured to herself: "I really believe that I begin to see how it was done. I am sure that if I undid it, I could do it up again afterwards."

She took the golden knot in her fingers, and was soon busily engaged in attempting to undo it. Meanwhile, the bright sunshine came through the open window, as did likewise the merry voices of the children, playing at a distance, and perhaps the voice of Epimetheus among them. Pandora stopped to listen. What a beautiful day it was! Would it not be wiser if she were to let the troublesome knot alone, and think no more about the box, but run and join her little playfellow and be happy?

All this time, however, her fingers were half unconsciously busy with the knot, and just then, by the merest accident, she gave the knot a kind of twist. The gold cord untwined itself, as if by magic, and left the box without a fastening.

Suddenly Pandora seemed to hear the murmur of small voices within. "Let us out, dear Pandora – pray, let us out!"

'What can it be?' thought Pandora. 'Is there something alive in the box? Maybe I should take a peep – just one peep – and then the lid shall be shut down as safely as ever! There cannot possibly be any harm in having just one little peep!'

As Pandora raised the lid, the cottage grew very dark and dismal, for a black cloud had swept quite over the sun, and seemed to have buried it alive. There had for a little while past been a low growling and muttering,

24

which all at once
broke into a heavy
peal of thunder.
But Pandora,
heeding nothing of
all this, lifted the lid
nearly upright, and
looked inside. It seemed
as if a sudden swarm of
winged creatures brushed past her, taking
flight out of the box. At the same instant,
she heard Epimetheus's footsteps
returning and he cried out as if he
were in pain. "Oh, I am stung!
Pandora, why have you opened
this wicked box?"

Pandora let fall the lid, and,
starting up, looked about her, to
see what had befallen Epimetheus.
The thunder cloud had so darkened

the room that she could not very clearly discern what was in it. But as her eyes grew more accustomed to the imperfect light, she saw a crowd of ugly little shapes, with bats' wings, looking horribly spiteful, and armed with long stings in their tails. It was one of these that had stung Epimetheus. Nor was it a great while before Pandora herself was stung and she too began to scream in pain.

The ugly things which had made their escape out of the box were the whole family of earthly Troubles. There were evil Passions, there were a great many species of Cares, there were more than a hundred and fifty Sorrows, there were Diseases (in a vast number of miserable and painful shapes), there were more kinds of Naughtiness than it would be of any use to talk about. And now the evil Troubles flew out of the windows and doors, to pester and torment the children all over the world – who from that moment on began to grow old and die.

Meanwhile, Epimetheus sat down sullenly in a

corner while Pandora flung herself upon the floor, sobbing as if her heart would break.

Then there was a little tap on the inside of the lid.

"What can that noise be?" cried Pandora.

Epimetheus made no answer.

Again the tap! It sounded like the tiny knuckles of a fairy's hand, knocking lightly on the inside of the box. "Let me out!" came a sweet voice. "I am not like those wicked creatures that have stings in their tails. They are no brothers and sisters of mine, as you would see at once, if you were only to get a glimpse of me. Come, come, my pretty Pandora! I am sure you will let me out!"

"Shall I lift the lid again?" whispered Pandora to Epimetheus.

"Just as you please," replied the boy. "You have done so much mischief already, that perhaps you may as well do a little more. One other Trouble, in such a swarm as you have set adrift about the world, can make no very great difference."

So the two children again lifted the lid. Out flew a sunny and smiling little personage, and hovered about the room. She flew to Epimetheus, and laid the least touch of her finger on the inflamed spot where the Trouble had stung him, and immediately the anguish of it was gone. Then she kissed Pandora on the forehead, and her hurt was cured likewise.

"Who are you, beautiful creature?" enquired Pandora, shyly.

"I am called Hope!" answered the sunshiny figure. "I was packed into the box, to make amends to the human race for that swarm of ugly Troubles, which was destined to be let loose among them. Never fear – we shall do pretty well in spite of them all."

"And will you stay with us," asked Epimetheus, "for ever and ever?"

"As long as you need me," said Hope, "and that will be as long as you live in the world – I promise never to desert you."

And she never has.

Peter and the Magic Goose

From *Fairy Stories and Fables*
by James Baldwin

THERE WAS ONCE a man who had three sons. The eldest of these sons was called Jacob, the second John, and the youngest Peter. Now Peter was good-natured and not very wise, and so it was easy for his brothers to play tricks on him. When there was hard work to be done, it was Peter that had to do it, and when anything went wrong about the farm, it was Peter that had to bear the blame for it.

One day in summer Jacob wanted to go into the woods to cut down a tree. So his mother gave him a nice cake and a bottle of milk for lunch, and told him that as soon as he felt tired he must come home and let Peter finish the job.

While he was looking at the trees and wondering which one to cut down, a little red-faced man came along. He seemed to be very old and feeble, and he said to Jacob: "Kind sir, will you not give me a piece of that nice cake which is in your pocket? I have not had anything to eat since yesterday."

"Not a bit of it," said Jacob. "I have nothing for beggars. If you want food, you must work for it as I do."

The little man said not a word but hobbled away, and Jacob began to chop his tree. He had hardly made a dozen strokes when his foot slipped. He fell against his axe and cut his arm so badly that he had to go home to have it bound.

The next day John said that he would go out and finish cutting the tree. So his mother baked a nice cake for him, and gave him a bottle of milk for his lunch, and told him to take care and not hurt himself.

John had hardly reached the wood, when he met the little red-faced man, hobbling along among the trees. "Please give me a bite of the nice cake and let me have a taste of the milk in that bottle," said the man, "for I am almost dead with hunger and thirst."

"Why should I give you anything?" said John, "I have no more than I want for myself."

The little man made no answer, and John walked on through the woods, until he found the tree which his brother had begun to chop down. At the very first stroke, his axe glanced and struck his foot, and cut so deep a gash that the blood rushed out in a stream. Some men who were not far off heard his cries and came to him, and if they had not bound his wound and carried him home, he would have died.

The next day Peter's mother said: "Peter, do you see what you have made your brothers suffer by your idleness? If you had gone into the woods as you should have done in the first place, this would not have happened. So take the axe and go now, and don't come home till you have cut that tree down." And then she gave him a hard crust of bread, and a small flask of sour milk for his lunch.

It was a long time before Peter found the tree, and when he came to it, he was both hungry and tired. He took the crust of bread from his pocket and was just going to taste it, when the little red-faced man stood before him. "Please give me one crumb of your bread and a drop of your milk in, for I am dying of hunger and thirst," said the poor man.

"Come and sit down with me on this log," said Peter, "and I will share it all with you."

So the two sat together, side by side, and ate their lunch, and Peter thought that he had never tasted anything so good.

When they had finished, the little man said: "You are very kind-hearted, so I'll tell you a secret. When you have cut the tree down, look in the hollow stump. There you will find a strange creature which you must carry to the king. It may be that some people will try to touch the creature as you are walking along, and so you must be sure whenever it cries out, to say, 'Hold fast! Hold fast! Hold fast!'"

After the little man had gone on his way, Peter took up his axe and began to chop with all his might. The chips flew, and it was not long till the tree began to tremble, and soon it fell with a crash to the ground. There was a round hollow place in the stump, and in it sat – a goose.

Peter thought that this was not a very strange creature after all, for he had seen geese all his life. If he had been wiser, he would have laughed at the idea of carrying it to the king, but, since the little man had told him to do so, he picked the goose up in his arms and started at once.

He made his way out of the woods, and soon came to the great road which led to the king's town. By the side of the road there was an inn, and some men were standing in the wagon yard nearby. When Peter came up with the goose in his arms, the innkeeper's daughter, who was looking out at the door, called to him, and said: "Where did you get that pretty goose? You'll give me one of its feathers, won't you?"

"Come and pull one out," said Peter, kindly.

The girl ran out and tried to get one of the long white feathers from the bird's wing, but the moment that she touched it the goose screamed, and Peter remembered what the little man had told him to say. "Hold fast! Hold fast! Hold fast!" he cried, and the young lady's fingers stuck so fast to the goose that she could not let go. She screamed and tried her best to pull away, but Peter walked along and took no more notice of her at all.

The men who were standing in the yard laughed, for they thought that she was only making believe, but the stable boy, when he heard her cries, ran out into the road to see what was the matter.

"Oh, Tommy, Tommy help me!" cried the poor girl. "Give me your hand and set me free from this horrid goose."

"Of course I will," said Tommy, and he seized the girl's hand.

But at that very moment the goose screamed again, and Peter, without looking back, cried out: "Hold fast! Hold fast! Hold fast!"

The stable boy could not let go of the girl's hand, but was obliged to follow after her, and although he howled loudly and tried to pull away, Peter walked steadily along and seemed not to notice him.

They soon came to a village where there were many people out for a holiday. A circus show was about to open, and the clown was in the street doing some of his tricks. When he saw Peter and the girl and the stable boy passing by, he cried: "What's the matter? Have three more clowns come to town?"

"I am no clown," cried the stable boy, "but this girl holds my hand so tight that I can't get away. Set me free, and I will do you as good a turn some day."

The clown, in his droll way, seized the stable boy by the string of his apron. The goose screamed, and Peter cried out: "Hold fast! Hold fast! Hold fast!"

Of course the clown could not let go. But Peter walked on, and looked neither to the right nor to the left. When the people saw the clown trying to pull away, they thought he was only at his tricks again, and everybody laughed.

Just then the mayor of the village came walking up the street. He was a very grave, sober man who was never known to smile, and the clown's silly actions did not please him at all. "What do you mean by grinning at me?" he said, and he seized the fellow's coat tail and tried to stop him.

But at that moment the goose screamed, and Peter again cried out: "Hold fast! Hold fast! Hold fast!" What could the mayor do but follow Peter with the rest? For he could not let go.

The wife of the mayor was greatly vexed when she saw her husband marching along and hanging to the clown's coat tail. She ran after him and seized his free arm and tried her best to pull him away.

The goose screamed, and Peter, without looking back, cried out: "Hold fast! Hold fast! Hold fast!"

The good lady could not help herself. She had to walk along whether she would or not, and make the best of it. A great many people followed, laughing and wondering, but none of them wanted to touch the mayor's wife – for she kept her tongue going very fast, you may be sure.

In a little while, Peter came in sight of the king's palace. Just before reaching the gates he met a fine carriage drawn by four white horses, and in the carriage sat a young lady, but with a solemn look.

Peter and his train stepped aside to let the carriage pass. When the young lady saw the goose, and the way in which so many people had to walk behind it, she burst into a loud laugh. She ordered the coachman to stop, so that she might see better, and the longer she looked, the harder she laughed.

"The princess has laughed! The princess has laughed!" cried all the servants that were with her, and one of them ran back to tell the king about it.

When the king heard what had happened he was delighted. When he saw Peter and his train he was so amused that he laughed louder than anybody else.

"My good friend," he said to Peter, "which will you choose?"

Peter stared at him and said nothing, for he did not know what the king meant.

"Do you know what I promised to the one who would make my daughter laugh?" said the king.

"No, I don't think I do," said Peter.

"I promised a thousand dollars or a piece of land," said the king. "Which will you choose?"

"I think I'll take the land," said Peter.

He stroked the goose's head, and in a moment the girl and the stable boy and the clown and the mayor and the mayor's wife were suddenly free.

"What a pretty bird!" said the princess as she came to look at the goose. Then she reached out her pretty white hand to stroke its neck.

The goose screamed, and Peter cried out: "Hold fast! Hold fast! Hold fast!"

And the princess thought that Peter was the handsomest lad she had ever seen. The king, too, was pleased with him and gave him a fine suit of clothes, and took him into the palace to be a page and wait on the ladies at the table.

When Peter grew up to be a strong and handsome man, he became a brave knight, and he and the princess were married. But the goose flew up into the air and winged its way back to the forest, and nobody has seen it from that day to this.